QUIMBLE WOOD

QUIMBLE WOOD

by N. M. Bodecker

illustrated by Branka Starr

A MARGARET K. MCELDERRY BOOK

Atheneum   1981   New York

Library of Congress Cataloging in Publication Data

Bodecker, N M
Quimble Wood.
"A Margaret K. McElderry book."
SUMMARY: Four quimbles, each no bigger than a little
finger, fall out of a car in a forest where they must
learn to fend for themselves quickly since winter is not
far off.
I. Starr, Branka. II. Title.
PZ7.B63514Qi   [E]   80-24045

ISBN 0-689-50190-0

Text copyright © 1981 by N. M. Bodecker
Illustrations copyright © 1981 by Branka Starr
Published simultaneously in Canada by
McClelland & Stewart, Ltd.
Composition by American–Stratford Graphic Services, Inc.
Brattleboro, Vermont
Printed by Halliday Lithograph Corporation
West Hanover, Massachusetts
Bound by A. Horowitz & Son
Fairfield, New Jersey
First Edition

QUIMBLE WOOD

1
THE FOUR POSTER

There once were four quimbles in a box, Quilliam, Quilice, Quint and the unstoppable Quenelope, each wearing a tall, pointed hat, and each no bigger than your little finger.

The box dropped out of a bag that dropped out of a car, where the road from Glumsea Sands to Nutwold-in-the-Thicket winds through the forest. The car stopped, and the bag was recovered, but no one noticed that the quimble box was missing. It had gotten under some ferns, the lid had come off, and the quimbles had rolled into the grass at the edge of a ditch.

Because it was fall, and the quimbles were the color of leaves and grasses, no one saw them. And because their voices were so tiny, no one heard them, though they cried: "Here we are!" as loudly as they could.

So the car drove off without them, and that's how the quimbles came to be in the woods.

They sat down in the grass together in the late afternoon sun, between the dirt road and the forest, wondering what would happen to them now. They had never been in the woods before, and suddenly it looked as if they would be there forever. They decided to spend the night near the road, hoping that in the morning someone would come looking for them, though in their hearts they knew that no one would.

They pushed the box in deeper among the ferns, stuck the lid on four sticks over it, like a canopy, and when it got dark, snuggled into the cotton wool.

The night was full of unfamiliar sounds. Things sniffed and scratched and rustled about. A fox barked. Owls chased each other — "Woo-woo! Woo-w-h-o-o-o-! Woo-woo! woo-w-h-o-o-o-!" — deeper and deeper into the woods. And high above their canopy the wind surged through the top of the forest. The quimbles pulled the covers over their heads, and hugged each other, and listened . . . and fell asleep.

But during the night the sky grew dark, and wind and rain

came crashing through the forest. The quimbles burrowed deeper into the cotton, but the rain blew under the canopy right into their bed. Long before daybreak they were drenched and their bed was coming unglued. The canopy leaked and sagged. Finally a wild gust of wind carried it off into the dark. All they could do was turn their ruined bed upside down, crawl under it, and wait for morning.

At first light they left it to look for shelter in the forest. But between the ferns and the trees ran the ditch. Rain had turned it into a raging river, and beyond it towered a stone wall, like a mountain, so wild and dark that they almost lost heart.

But Quilliam (who knew about such things) got them across the river on a fallen branch, white water rushing below, gusts of wind tugging fiercely at their tall hats. Quilice (who could climb) and Quenelope (who didn't mind dark, narrow places) led them up the stone wall, through crevices as dark as drains, into the rainy woods. Quint (who had hurt his knee) hobbled along, furious when they helped him and quite helpless when they didn't.

It was a sad little party that trudged on in the rain. Water was everywhere: puddles as big as lakes, raindrops the size of quimbles' noses. Water ran from their hats down their cold backs into their squelching boots. Halfway through the afternoon, they sat down on a rock hungry and cold, almost ready to give up.

And that's when Quenelope called them "a miserable bunch of quillipips."

No one had called them that before. And NO ONE, they would make sure, would ever call them that again. For a

quillipip is a sniffy-snively-self-pitying little simper-simon of a squimble. And who wants to be that? So they wiped their wet noses angrily on their wet sleeves and went on.

Snails crossed their path. Salamanders watched them from the rocks. A few late mosquitoes came out of the fog to attack them, but withdrew disgustedly to their dank places when they found that you cannot draw blood from a quimble.

Day after day they traveled through the forest, living off brambles and wild raspberries. Quilice shimmied up the bushes and brought berries down in her hat.

At night they built shelters of sticks and leaves, but never felt quite warm, never found quite the right place to settle, and the rain kept returning as if it could never quite finish the job.

Late one afternoon, after struggling uphill in the rain for hours, they came to a large old tree. At the foot between the roots was a dark opening, like the entrance to a cave.

They stopped, but since what might be inside couldn't be much worse than what was outside, in they went.

2
THE HOLLOW TREE

Inside it was dark as night and smelled of dry rot. But to the quimbles it was the most welcoming house. They wrung out their clothes, stuffed them with moss to dry, and buried themselves in the leaves.

It was so nice to be warm that for a time they thought of nothing else. Just snuggled deeper into the leaves, giggling.

But when the giggling stopped, they had a strange, uneasy feeling that someone or something was watching them. They sat quite still, straining ears and eyes. And then they saw it. A thin, quivering snout. Long, quivering whiskers. Large, shining eyes, and huge, rounded ears.

A mouse. A small, black-eyed mouse, but to them as large as a bear.

The mouse sat, watching them suspiciously. It had never seen quimbles before and didn't know what they were. And the quimbles sat watching the mouse. Suddenly Quenelope said: "Maybe it's as afraid of us as we are of it." Quilliam said, "Are you?" The mouse said, "Yes," and they were talking as if they had known each other forever.

The quimbles told the mouse all that had happened to them, and the mouse listened attentively. When they came to the long hike through the rainy forest it said: "Awful thing being wet. And hungry too . . . sometimes at the end of winter, when my stores run out . . . But, my dear little people," said the mouse interrupting herself, "*you* must be hungry right now."

In a flash she was gone. In a flash she was back carrying food from her storerooms. "There! Let me open you a nut, I have the opener right here," she said, showing her sharp little teeth.

When they had eaten, they talked about tomorrow, about keeping warm and dry, and about a place to live. "You could live with me," said the mouse a little doubtfully, "at least for a while." She was a fussy housekeeper and didn't fancy a mousehole-full of quimbles. But if they *really* needed her . . .

The quimbles said, "Thank you," but being people they didn't think they would take to living underground. What they *really* needed was a house. The mouse felt much relieved and began telling them about the woods: where to find the last berries and the best nuts, where the wild onions

grew, and where there was a garden by the pond, with tomatoes ripening just before frost, as if she could think only of food. "But I know about being hungry," she said. "A terrible thing. You scrounge around all day in the snow and find nothing. I know about being cold too. Once during a thaw my house filled with water. Then it froze . . ." "But I mustn't talk. Time I got on with my work," and she slipped away into the forest.

The quimbles had listened carefully, winter was only a few short weeks away, and there was so much to be done — things they had never had to think of before. Food for the snowy months ahead. Firewood to keep them warm. Logs for a house. Rocks for a fireplace. Beds, winter clothes, snowshoes, pots and pans. A place to build their house. "We could build right here under the tree," said Quint.

But that night the mouse told them about snowdrifts: "Many times as high as a quimble-house. You would be buried. If I were you, I should build in a tree." A tree house. It sounded nice. But when they thought of getting everything up into a tree, logs, rocks and stores, it seemed an endless undertaking. As if just finding the logs wasn't enough.

"Logs?" asked the mouse. And when they explained what they meant, her eyes grew big and bright. "Beaver sticks!" she said, and that was all she *would* say. "I cannot explain. It's too difficult, but I'll show you in the morning."

3
BEAVER BEACH

Bright and early the mouse led them down through the blueberry bushes to a tiny sandy beach on the pond. All along the shore, the water was full of sticks, some as big as an elephant's trunk, some no thicker than a quimble's wrist, all stripped of their bark, as clean as new-cut timber.

"Beaver Beach," said the mouse. "The beavers come at night to eat bark off trees they fell in the woods. They cut them into sticks to make them easier to carry."

Sticks to the beavers perhaps, but to the quimbles they were a log-jam. More logs than they would ever need. They thanked the mouse and set to work. Quilliam and Quenelope dragged logs out of the pond. Quilice broke thorns off a rose bush and hammered them into a tree, one above the other, as steps to an abandoned vireo's nest, where they would live while they built their house and sheds on some large, flat fungi growing out of the tree.

Quint, who was good at finding things, went into the woods looking for whatever might be useful, hoping to find an old dump from an abandoned camp. They worked quietly all day. By sunset enough lumber for a house was drying on the beach, Quilice had finished the steps, and Quint had returned, carrying a ragged piece of glass for a window wrapped in a small piece of cloth, and a larger piece of cloth rolled up like a carpet.

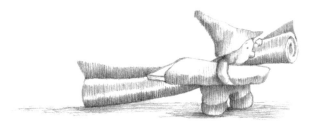

They put the small piece in the bottom of the nest to keep out drafts, tied the large piece overhead for a roof, and had a blueberry supper in bed. They cut the blueberries in two like melons with a piece of clam shell, scooped the inside out with their hands, and drank water out of hexagonal cups made from a honeycomb. When the mouse came at dusk, they were fast asleep, snoring the thin, high-pitched snores of contented quimbles.

The nights were cool but without frost. The days were the cloudless days of Indian summer. The quimbles worked hard and late. "We have all winter for sitting around," said Quenelope, "but if we aren't ready before snow, we'll be sorry." They knew that well enough, but on sunny days, when dragonflies and bluets skimmed over the water, it was hard to believe it would ever be different.

Still the piles under the tree grew. Logs, rocks, ash-tree-seed shingles, grass for making ropes, pine needles for weaving mats and baskets. Clay for cement, moss for caulking, flag stones for the hearth. Every night Quint returned from his dump-picking with new treasures, arranging them in neat piles under an old sasparilla. Quint's Piles, they called them. They rummaged through them and usually found what they needed.

But when they were ready to build, they had no saw. The mouse offered to cut the logs with her teeth, but they knew she didn't really have the time. Quint searched his dump for days, but found nothing useable. One morning he went off looking very grim indeed. He didn't go to the dump. Instead they heard him hammering in the woods, doing something mysterious with sticks and rocks and pitch from a pine tree. But they left him alone, and just before dark Quint came home with a two-handed saw made from a bit of rusty tin. It was no beauty, the handles were held on with pitch and string, but it worked. Quilliam and Quenelope used it. And

the next day he made another for Quilice and himself.

These were their happiest days, when the house began taking shape. They had grass-seed cereal with honey for breakfast, served in cherry-pip poringers, and kept an acorn bowl of blueberries within reach when they worked. Quilliam did the heavy carpentry. Quenelope built the chimney. Quint

fitted windows and doors. Quilice built ladders from one plat-
form to another. Together they raised the roof, hung the
shingles, made the food and tidied things up at the end of
the day.

The mouse came every night to watch their progress and
was very pleased indeed.

4
THE FIRE

Then the weather turned cold. One morning they woke up, shivering in woods white with frost. When they came down to the pond to wash, ice had formed at the edge, and the water was covered with bright leaves fallen during the night.

They stood on the beach, holding hands, watching the white mist and the still water. This wasn't winter, but it was the first warning. They could see their breath in the air as they worked, their hands became numb, and they shivered in their thin clothes.

They began feeling almost as hopeless as on their first

morning in the woods. The roof was only half shingled, the stores weren't half in, the chimney wasn't finished. They had neither firewood nor winter clothes. They watched the stars over the vireo's nest at night and thought they looked like bits of ice growing closer and closer together, as if the skies were freezing over like the pond.

With flint and touchwood, they made a fire on the beach to warm their hands. But when they put it out at night, the nest seemed colder than ever. They stuffed their clothes with down, but it tickled and made sleep difficult.

One frosty evening, they brought clay up from the beach, flattened it on the floor of the nest, put stones around it and built a fire. How nice it felt. They piled on more wood and sat around it telling stories and singing. They hadn't been so warm in weeks. In a while they would put out the fire and go to sleep, but for a few more minutes they would enjoy the warmth and the light.

They were all very tired and as they sat looking into the

flames, their heads nodded, and their eyes closed . . .

Suddenly — they didn't know how it happened — the fire was no longer in the hearth, but in the nest. One moment they were nodding around a friendly glow, the next they were out on the branch watching angry flames leaping out everywhere, burning through the ties holding the nest to the branch, and the nest dropping like a ball of fire into the leaves on the forest floor.

They raced down ladders and steps to the ground. The nest had flared up quickly and was gone, but a ring of flames was spreading in the leaves. Quint and Quenelope stamped out as many as they could with their feet. Quilliam and Quilice brought water up from the pond in their hats. Long after the last spark was gone they poured water on the black circle, and they took turns watching it through the night.

Quilice took the last watch. She sat huddled in a piece of sack cloth looking out over the water as day broke, tired and sad.

If the quimbles had thought that the mouse would feel sorry for them, now that they had nowhere to sleep, they were very much mistaken.

When the mouse came by that morning, she was furious. News of the fire had spread long before dawn, because of all the dread things that threaten the forest — floods, hurricanes, blizzards and droughts — none is as dreadful as a forest fire. It leaves nothing: no food, no shelter, no life. The mouse told them this, and much more, in a low shaky voice full of anger and fear. And when the quimbles said they were sorry, she said only, "You should be," and went away.

5
QUIMBLE WOOD

The quimbles talked little that day and when they made a bed for the night in their unfinished house, they cried. Not because they felt sorry for themselves, but because the woods had given them shelter, and they had done something thoughtless that might have hurt the woods and had made the mouse angry. Perhaps they also cried a little because they were tired and cold and everything was so difficult. But they hugged each other and talked. Cried a little more. And blew their noses and smiled and went to sleep. And during the night the mouse, who felt sorry in her own way for having had to be so angry, left a small pile of nuts at the foot of their tree.

That day Quint dragged home two half milkweed pods he

—had found. They used them for beds. Probably the first time anyone put beds in a house before the roof was on.

In the next few days they finished shingling, filled cracks in the walls with clay, and lined the inside with birch bark. They combed the old garden for what had been left and brought in their last stores.

The night they built the first fire in their fireplace the mouse came to visit. They showed her their storehouses, and she admired everything. Honeycombs of jam and honey. Bits of pears and apples drying on grass ropes. Bins of tiny potatoes and carrots stored in maple leaves. Brussels sprouts in hay. Baskets of grain for flour. Chokecherries in bundles.

Wild onions in nets. Bunches of feathers and down for feather beds and down parkas. Wintergreen hanging from the rafters. Sheds full of firewood and kindling, and a bath house with a clam shell for a tub.

After supper they sat by the fire talking about all the things they would make, and do, and build during the winter. The mouse went home late, certain that her little people were safe and sound. But before she left, Quenelope tugged gently at her whiskers and called her "a dear old bear," which the mouse thought nice, if perhaps a little exaggerated.

At last the quimbles were settled in a house of their own. They called it Quimble Wood because it was in the woods and quimbles lived in it. Now the snows could come for all they cared, and late one afternoon, when a fire crackled in the fireplace, the first snowflake landed on their window. A large snowflake, nearly as big as the little window. It seemed to flutter, as if it had wings and wanted to come into the room with the bright fire.

When they looked more closely, they saw that it was a white moth, shivering with cold. They brought it inside, to let it warm itself by the fire. And all winter it lived with them at Quimble Wood as their pet.

But that is another story for another day.